Karen's Roller Skates

Also in the Babysitters Little Sister series:

Karen's Witch

Karen's Worst Day

Karen's Kittycat Club

Look out for:

Karen's School Picture

Karen's Little Sister

Karen's Roller Skates
Ann M. Martin

Illustrations by Susan Tang

Hippo Books
Scholastic Children's Books
London

This book is in
loving memory of my grandmother
Adele Read Martin
August 2, 1894 − April 18, 1988

Scholastic Children's Books,
Scholastic Publications Ltd,
7-9 Pratt Street, London NW1 0AE, UK

Scholastic Inc.,
730 Broadway, New York, NY 10003, USA

Scholastic Canada Ltd,
123 Newkirk Road, Richmond Hill,
Ontario, Canada L4C 3G5

Ashton Scholastic Pty Ltd,
P O Box 579, Gosford, New South Wales,
Australia

Ashton Scholastic Ltd,
Private Bag 1, Penrose, Auckland,
New Zealand

First published in the US by Scholastic Inc., 1988
First published in the UK by Scholastic Publications Ltd, 1992

Text copyright © Ann M. Martin, 1988

ISBN 0 590 55008 X

Typeset by A.J. Latham Ltd, Dunstable, Beds
Printed by Cox & Wyman Ltd, Reading, Berks

BABYSITTERS LITTLE SISTER is a trademark of Scholastic Inc.

10 9 8 7 6 5 4 3 2

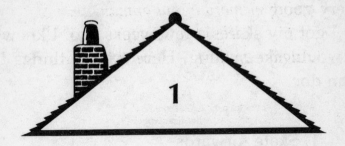

Daredevil

"Look out! Look out! I'm coming through!"
I shouted.

I was on my new roller skates, skating
very fast.

My little brother Andrew and my friend
Nancy Dawes were on the pavement. They
weren't on roller skates, so it was easier for
them to jump out of my way than for me to
stop.

My name is Karen Brewer, and I'm almost
seven. I'm a world champion skater. Well,
maybe not a *world* champion skater. Well,

maybe not a champion at all. But I am very, very good.

I got my skates a few weeks ago. I knew I would like skating. Here are the things I can do:

1. Skate forwards
2. Skate forwards fast
3. Skate backwards (not so fast)
4. Turn around
5. Stop without falling down
6. Try lots of stunts.

Actually I'm not really allowed to do number six. I can do *some* stunts, but my parents don't like me to try dangerous ones. Daddy says "You're a daredevil, Karen. Be careful when you're skating. We don't want any broken bones."

Maybe I am a daredevil. I like trying stunts. I like trying to jump and spin. I like leaping over things. I like flying over bumps in the pavement.

When I'm skating I wear shorts with a stripe up each leg; red-and-white-striped socks; a red-and-white jumper; a red headband; wrist guards; knee pads; and of course, my skates.

My skates are really great. They are red with yellow wheels and they lace up.

I love my skates.

"I'm coming through!" I yelled again.

Nancy and Andrew jumped out of the way. We have had a couple of small accidents. Maybe that's why Daddy calls me a daredevil. Maybe that's why he warns me to be careful.

I try to remember to be careful, but sometimes I forget. It is fun to go fast. It is fun to jump. When I go fast, I feel like I'm flying. When I try a new stunt, I feel breathless and happy.

"Karen! Andrew! Time to come in!" That was our mother.

"Nancy! Time for you to come in, too." That was Mrs Dawes. Nancy lives next door to Mummy's house.

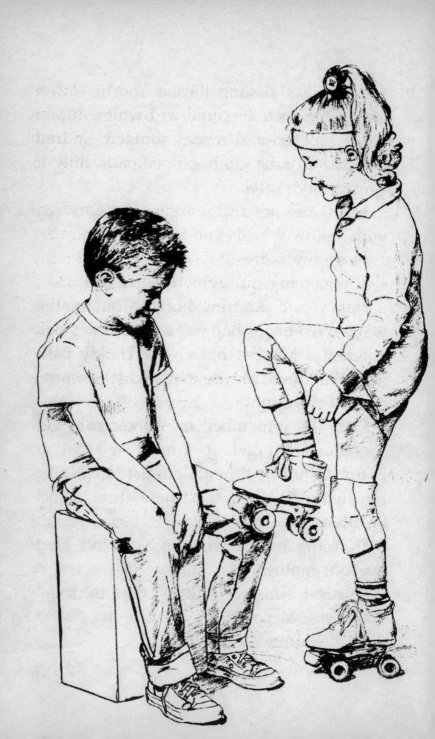

It was a Thursday afternoon. Mrs Dawes wanted Nancy to come in because it was time for dinner. Mummy wanted Andrew and me to come in because it was time to go to Daddy's.

My mummy and daddy are divorced. Andrew and I live at our daddy's every other weekend and for two weeks in the summer. The rest of the time we live at our mummy's. Usually we go to Daddy's on Friday afternoon. But that weekend we were going a day early. Mummy and Seth were going on holiday. (Seth is our stepfather.) They were going to Maine for three days.

" 'Bye, Nancy," I said. "See you in school tomorrow."

" 'Bye, Karen. 'Bye Andrew," Nancy replied.

I skated up my driveway as fast as I could go. Andrew ran behind me. We were sorry we weren't going to Maine. But going to Daddy's was almost as good. I would bring my skates with me.

I was looking forward to a weekend of roller-skating.

There was a new stunt I wanted to try.

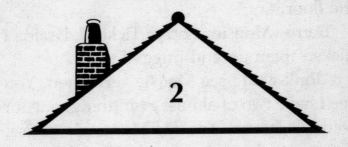

Saturday Morning

Stretch, stretch, stretch.

Yawn.

Sometimes it's hard to wake up. But not on a Saturday morning. On a Saturday morning you can roll around in bed. You can scrunch up the pillow. You can kiss your stuffed animals. But you don't have to get up unless you want to.

I lay in my bed. I was sooooo happy it was Saturday. I kicked the duvet off. Then I looked around for Moosie, my stuffed cat, and Tickly, my blanket. I found them on the floor.

"Sorry, Moosie. Sorry, Tickly," I said. I picked them up and hugged them.

I don't get to see Moosie very often. You see I have two of almost everything, one for Daddy's house, one for Mummy's house. This is so that when Andrew and I go to Daddy's, we hardly have to bring anything with us. Since Moosie stays at Daddy's, I only see him every other weekend. Andrew

and I have clothes and toys and books at Daddy's, too. We have other clothes and toys and books at Mummy's. (Actually, for a long time, I had only one Tickly. But I forgot Tickly so many times going back and forth between Mummy's and Daddy's, that finally I just ripped him in half. Now I have half of Tickly at the big house and half of Tickly at the little house.)

The big house is Daddy's. It really is a big house and lots of people live there. Daddy and my stepmother, Elizabeth, live there as well as Elizabeth's four children. Sam and Charlie are really grown-up and go to high school. Kristy is younger then they are — she's thirteen. She babysits for me. I love Kristy and I'm really glad she's my big sister. David Michael is a bit older than I am. He's seven. As soon as I have birthday, I'll catch up with him.

Guess who else lives in the big house? Shannon and Boo-Boo. Shannon is David Michael's puppy. Well, she's really everybody's puppy, but she's *mostly* David

Michael's. Boo-Boo is Daddy's fat old cat. I don't like him very much. He doesn't do anything except eat, sleep, meow, and claw the furniture.

Do you want to hear something scary? Next door to the big house lives a witch. Really! Cross my heart. Most people think she is just an old woman named Mrs Porter. But I know she is a witch. Her witch's name is Morbidda Destiny. She has a strange cat called Midnight. She grows magic herbs in her back garden. And several times I've seen her with a broom.

My big-house best friend is Hannie Papadakis. She lives across the road from us. Hannie and Nancy Dawes and I are in the same class at school. (Since we go to a private school and David Michael goes to a state school, I only see him every other weekend. He can be a pain, so I don't mind this too much.)

The little house is Mummy's. It really is a little house, and the only people who live there are Mummy and Seth and Andrew and me. Seth has a dog called Midgie and a cat called Rocky.

Nancy Dawes is my little-house best friend.

I like all the people at both houses, and *most* of the animals. So does Andrew. But sometimes we wish that our parents weren't divorced and that we lived in just one house.

"Then I could see you every day," I said to Moosie.

At last I got up. I put on my skating clothes and ran downstairs to eat my breakfast. It was a beautiful day and I wanted to try my new roller-skating stunt.

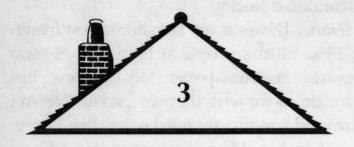

Oops!

As soon as breakfast was over, I put on my skates. I don't have two pairs of skates, and I don't have two sets of skating clothes. So I have to remember to bring my skates and skating clothes with me when I go to Mummy's or to Daddy's.

I'm not allowed to wear my roller skates indoors. That is a rule at both the big house and the little house.

I carried my skates outdoors and sat down on the steps in front of the house. I put one foot in one skate.

"Karen!" called Elizabeth.

"Yes?" I answered. "I'm out at the front."

Elizabeth came to the door. She was holding Shannon's lead. "Darling, would you take Shannon for a walk, please?"

I didn't know what to do. I was getting ready to go skating, but I wanted to walk Shannon, too. Then I had an idea.

"Yes!" I replied.

Elizabeth handed me the lead. I took off my skate and came back inside.

"Thanks, Karen," said Elizabeth.

"You're welcome. . . . Hey, Andrew!" I called.

Andrew came running.

"Do you want to help me walk Shannon?" I asked him. "I've got a great idea. I know how we can walk Shannon, *and* I can roller-skate, *and* you can ride your trike."

"How?" asked Andrew.

"Like this." I fastened Shannon's lead to her collar. Then I gave the lead to my brother. "You can ride your trike and let Shannon run beside you," I told him. "I'll skate in

13

front of you so that Shannon doesn't get tangled up with me. Okay?"

"Okay," said Andrew.

We got Andrew's trike out of the garage. He sat on it and I gave him Shannon's lead.

Then I sat on the pavement and put my skates on. I remembered that I had left my wrist guards in the house. Oh, well, I thought, I don't really need them.

"Ready, steady, go!" I cried.

I charged down the pavement. Andrew was behind me. He travelled more slowly and Shannon ran next to him. Andrew was careful to keep Shannon away from the wheels of his trike.

ZOOM! I whizzed along until I was freewheeling. I saw a bump in the pavement ahead of me. Oh good! I thought as I sailed over it. Maybe someday I will be a skier and go flying through the air from ski jumps.

When I reached the driveway of the house next door, I skidded to a halt. Andrew stopped behind me.

"Woof!" said Shannon.

14

Andrew and I turned round. I skated back to our driveway. Suddenly I remembered the stunt I wanted to try.

"Hey, Andrew!" I said. "Do you want to see a really great stunt?"

"Yes!" replied Andrew. He loves stunts.

"Okay," I said. "I'll be right back."

I skated into our garage. On a shelf I found two empty coffee jars. Perfect. I skated back to the pavement and put the jars down next to each other.

"I," I announced to Andrew, "am going to leap over these jars. I saw a woman on TV do it. She leaped over *six*. But I will try just two."

"Oh, Karen," said Andrew. "Do you think you should?" He had stopped his trike and was sitting still. He looked very worried.

I felt a bit nervous myself. But I had to try the stunt. I backed away from the jars. Then I skated forwards as fast as I could. When I got near the jars, I jumped up, soared over them, and landed on my feet. I could hardly believe it.

16

"I did it!" I shouted.

"Hurray!" yelled Andrew.

I turned around to grin at him. That was when I lost my balance. My feet shot out from under me. I put my hands out as I fell. I landed on them hard.

"Ow, ow, ow!" I cried. "Andrew, I'm hurt!"

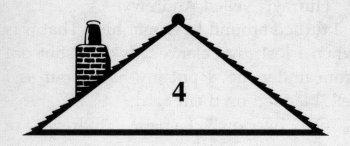

Broken Wrist

My bottom hurt where I'd sat down on it. But my right wrist hurt more. I looked at it.

I screamed.

My wrist was bent back at a funny angle. I couldn't wiggle my fingers. When I tried to move my wrist, it hurt so much I gasped.

"Andrew, my wrist is hurt!" I cried.

Andrew jumped off his trike. He and Shannon ran to me. When he saw my wrist, he began to cry. "Oh, Karen!" he said.

"Get Daddy," I whispered to him.

Andrew left Shannon with me to keep me company. Then he ran into the house. I had never seen him run so fast.

I sat on the pavement and tried not to look at my wrist. I couldn't help crying, though. Shannon put her paws on my shoulder and licked my tears away.

"Thank you, Shannon," I said in a wavery voice.

"Karen!" Daddy called. He and Kristy came running out of the house. Daddy reached me first. He took one look at my wrist. Then he gathered me into his arms very gently.

"Does this hurt? Does this hurt?" he asked as he picked me up.

Daddy walked carefully back into the house. Kristy held onto my left hand, the one that wasn't hurt.

"I should have worn my wrist guards," I said. I sniffled loudly.

"Don't worry about that now," said Daddy.

Elizabeth met us at the front door. She held it open and Daddy carried me inside. He laid me on the sofa in the living room.

"I think her wrist is broken," said Daddy.

Elizabeth looked pale. "I think you're right. I'll phone Doctor Dellenkamp."

While Elizabeth rang the doctor, Daddy and Kristy and Andrew sat with me on the sofa. Kristy was still holding my hand. She made me smile by singing a song about a baby bumblebee.

Soon Elizabeth came back.

"Karen, darling," she said, "Doctor

Dellenkamp wants you to go to hospital. She'll meet us in casualty. Kristy, you stay here with Andrew and David Michael. Sam and Charlie are out."

"No," said Kristy firmly. "I'm going to hospital with Karen."

Kristy and her mother looked at each other for a long time.

At last Elizabeth said, "Okay. You go. I'll stay here."

"Thanks, Mum," said Kristy. She gave Elizabeth a kiss.

I like Elizabeth, but I was glad Kristy was coming to the hospital with us. She is the best, best big sister ever.

Daddy carried me out to Elizabeth's estate car. "We'll take this car," he said. "You can lie down in the back."

"And I'll sit with you," Kristy added.

Elizabeth covered me with a blanket. "I'll see you soon," she said. "I know everything will be all right. And don't try to be brave. Scream and yell and give Doctor Dellenkamp a hard time if you feel like it."

I managed to giggle. "Okay," I said. Sometimes Elizabeth is funny.

Daddy pulled out of the driveway. He pulled out so fast that the tyres squealed. Then he raced through Stoneybrook to the hospital.

"There's the emergency entrance!" Kristy called.

Daddy zoomed in. I began to feel scared. My wrist hurt. And I'd never been to a hospital before.

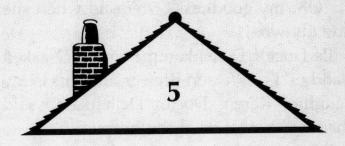

5

Emergency!

Daddy parked the car. He parked it near the wide double doors that were under the EMERGENCY sign. Then he carried me through the doors and down a hallway. Kristy walked with us.

"Did I ever tell you about the time I broke my ankle?" she asked.

I nodded. I was beginning to cry again. I didn't like the way the hospital smelled. It smelled of medicine; of horrid, nasty medicine.

Before Kristy could tell the story again,

23

we came to a desk. A lady was sitting behind it. "Oh, my goodness," she said when she saw my wrist.

"Is Doctor Dellenkamp here yet?" asked Daddy. "I'm Watson Brewer and this is my daughter Karen. Doctor Dellenkamp said she would meet us at the hospital."

"Here I am!"

I heard Dr Dellenkamp's voice in the hall behind us. Usually I don't like hearing her voice, because she is usually saying, "Okay, Karen, time for an injection." But this time I was glad to hear it. Dr Dellenkamp was going to make my wrist better.

That's what I thought. But the first thing she said was, "Karen, I won't be setting your wrist. We'll have to wait for the bone doctor. Fixing bones is what he does best. He should be here soon. While we're waiting for him, you can go to the X-ray room. We need some pictures of your wrist bones. And Mr Brewer, I need you to fill in some forms."

A nurse rolled a wheelchair over to us.

"Here is your chariot," she said to me. "And I am your chariot driver. I will take you to X-ray."

"All by myself?" I said. I wasn't sure what X-ray was, and I didn't want to go there. "Do I *have* to go?" I asked.

"Yes," Dr Dellenkamp told me. "Kristy can go with you. How would you like that."

Kristy looked at me. "Okay?" she said, "Your daddy has to fill in forms. Besides, I want to watch. I love hospitals."

I thought Kristy was crazy. But if she would come with me, I would go to X-ray. "Okay," I said.

Daddy put me in the wheelchair.

"Off we go," said the nurse. "When we're finished, I'll bring you back to your dad."

The nurse pushed me down a hallway. I had never sat in a wheelchair. Everyone in the hall looked at me. I began to feel quite important. The nurse pushed me into a little room with a lot of machines in it. There was a man wearing a white jacket and white trousers in the room. He looked like a doctor

25

— and not like a doctor. There was no stethoscope round his neck.

"Hallo," he said, "I'm Tom. I'm the X-ray technician. I'm going to take pictures of the inside of your wrist — of your wrist bones."

"Yuck," I said.

Tom rested my arm on a table. He covered me with an apron that felt very heavy.

"What's this for?" I asked.

"It's to protect you from the X-rays. We only want them near your wrist. Don't worry. I know what I'm doing."

Then he moved one of the machines right up to my wrist. *Click* went the machine.

"The biggest camera in the world," said Kristy, who was standing in the doorway, watching.

I giggled.

Tom started moving my arm around and taking more pictures. *Click*, *click*, *click*. Sometimes it hurt to move my arm, so Tom tried to be very careful. And I tried not to cry. Tom was nice.

26

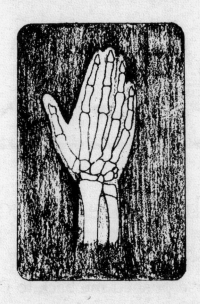

"All finished," Tom said soon. He took off the apron.

"Now what?" I asked.

"Your chariot will take you back to your father," said the nurse.

"Goodbye, Karen!" called Tom. "I hope you feel better soon."

"Goodbye," I replied. "Thank you."

It was time to wait for the bone doctor.

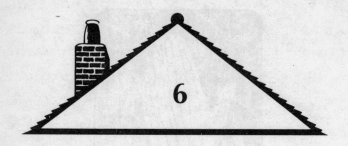

The Bone Doctor

The nurse pushed me back to Daddy.

"Tom took pictures of my bones," I told him. "Are you finished with those papers?"

"All finished," said Daddy.

Dr Dellenkamp showed us into a little room nearby. Well, it *felt* like a room, but it wasn't really one. The walls were just curtains. There was a long row of those rooms. You could pull the curtains open — or close them.

Dr Dellenkamp closed ours. She and Daddy helped me out of the wheelchair.

They sat me on a table that looked like a high bed. Then Dr Dellenkamp said, "The bone doctor will be here soon. His name is Doctor Humphrey. He's looking at your X-rays now, Karen. I'm going to go and look at them, too."

Dr Dellenkamp pushed through the curtains and left.

As soon as she had gone I said, "I'm bored."

Daddy and Kristy laughed.

Kristy told me three elephant jokes. Daddy began to sing a silly song about marching ants. But then the curtain opened. A man with a moustache came into the room.

"Are you the bone doctor?" I asked him.

"Yes," he replied. He smiled. "I'm Doctor Humphrey. You must be Karen Brewer."

Daddy introduced himself and Kristy. Then Dr Humphrey explained what he was going to do. I didn't like the sound of it. The very first thing was an injection.

"OW!" I screeched.

"All over," said Dr Humphrey. "Now

your wrist won't hurt for a while."

He and Daddy helped me to lie down. I began to feel very relaxed and a little sleepy. Dr Humphrey picked up my arm. It was the one with the broken wrist, but it didn't hurt a bit.

A tall pole was standing by the bed. There were some metal tubes hanging from it. The doctor put my fingers in them. When he let go, my fingers dropped down a little, but they stayed in the tubes. The tubes held them tight!

"That's great!" cried Kristy. She was watching my arm as it hung from the metal tubes. "I just saw all your bones go back where they belong. Your wrist doesn't look broken any more."

"That's right," said Dr Humphrey. "Now it's time to put the plastercast on."

Dr Humphrey wrapped cotton around and around my hand, my wrist, and right up over my elbow. Then he wrapped my arm with wet white bandages. The bandages dried fast. As they dried, they hardened into a plastercast. Dr Humphrey took my fingers out of the tubes and gave me my arm back. It weighed a ton. The plaster was *heavy*.

"How do you feel, Karen?" asked Daddy.

"Fine," I said. "A little sleepy."

"Good," said Dr Humphrey. "Now Tom just has to take a few more pictures of your wrist. We need to make sure the bones are in the right places. After that, you can go home."

So I visited Tom again, and the nurse pushed me around in my chariot again. When Tom had finished taking the pictures, Dr Dellenkamp talked to Daddy for a few minutes. Then she handed me a white sling. She rested my plaster in the bottom part and put the top part around my neck.

"Now your arm won't feel so heavy," she said.

The nurse wheeled me outside and Daddy drove the car over to us. He and Kristy helped me to lie down in the back.

I was still sleepy. And I was beginning to

get worried — how would I button buttons or feed Shannon and Boo-Boo or Rocky and Midgie with just one hand?

I began to feel very, very sorry for myself.

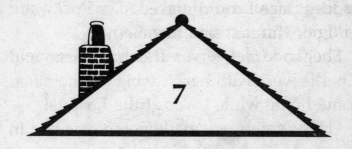

Tea and TV

Daddy steered the car into our driveway. Home again. He parked the car and then he came round to the back.

"Do you thing you can walk inside?" he asked me.

"No," I said crossly. "I'm too tired. And my arm hurts."

Daddy carried me into the house.

"Karen! Karen!" Andrew cried. He and David Michael opened the front door for us. "How's your wrist? Does it hurt? Did you cry? What did the doctor do?"

I showed them my plaster. I put on the saddest face I could make.

"Poor Karen," said Elizabeth.

She had met us in the hall. Sam and Charlie were with her. My big brothers had come home while I was at the hospital.

"Hey, Karen, we made you a nice bed in the study," said Sam.

"You can spend the rest of the afternoon there," added Charlie.

"Yes," said Andrew, "We put pillows there, and a blanket, and your books. We'll take care of you."

"I'll let Shannon stay with you," David Michael offered.

"Okay," I said in a small voice.

Daddy carried me into the study and laid me on the sofa. Kristy fluffed up my pillows. Elizabeth covered me with the blanket. Andrew handed me my favourite book, *The Witch Next Door*.

"Thank you," I said in my very small voice, "but I can't read this now. I don't feel well."

"How about phoning Mummy?" Daddy suggested. "That might make you feel better. We have to tell her about your accident, anyway."

So we rang Mummy in Maine. I talked to her for a long time. I told her about the hospital. Then I talked to Seth. When I hung up, I did feel better.

Sam and Charlie and Daddy and Elizabeth had left the room, but everyone else was still there. "What's on TV?" I asked.

David Michael jumped up, *"I'll* check," he said importantly. He found the remote control and switched the channels for me. We found some good cartoons.

"I'm hungry," I said after a while.

Kristy told Elizabeth, and Elizabeth made me a special lunch. She even made tea. For dessert, Charlie gave me a bar of chocolate.

"Wow!" I said. "Thanks."

All afternoon I played on the sofa. I didn't feel sleepy any more, and my wrist didn't hurt — much. I leaned against my pillows. I felt like a princess. I asked for hundreds of things.

But near tea-time when I said, "Hey Andrew, get me my colouring book," Andrew replied, "No. I'm busy."

"David Michael, *you* get my colouring book," I ordered.

"Get it yourself," he replied. "You can walk."

"Hmphh," I said. But I did get it myself. Only it wasn't any fun colouring with my left hand.

When tea was ready, Elizabeth said, "Come and sit with us at the table, Karen. It's tea-time."

"Can't I eat on the sofa?" I asked.

"Do you need to?"

"No." I was feeling fine.

Everyone must have known I was fine. After tea, David Michael got to watch *his* favourite programme on TV and Charlie didn't even give me another bar of chocolate.

By bedtime I was cross again. "I'm not

sleepy," I complained to Daddy and Elizabeth.

"Well, try going to sleep anyway," they replied.

So I did, even though I could only hold Tickly. Moosie had to rest beside me.

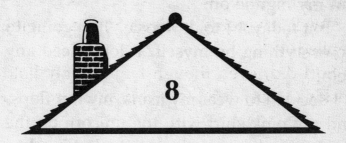

Back to Hospital

When I woke up the next morning, I didn't feel cross any more. I didn't feel sleepy and my wrist only hurt a little. Outside, the sun was shining.

"Well," I said to Moosie, "I'm not going to waste today lying around on a sofa. I'm going to play outside. There's nothing wrong with my legs. Maybe I could even go skating later."

I got out of bed. I took off my nightie. It wasn't easy, with only one hand. Last night,

Kristy had helped me to get undressed and put my nightie on.

"But today," I told Moosie, "I'm going to do everything by myself. I don't need any help."

I decided to wear my jeans, my flip-flops, and my pink shirt with the unicorn on the front. It took a long, long time, but I pulled on the jeans and the shirt.

"I did it!" I told Moosie. I felt as if I was two years old and just learning how to get dressed.

I slipped my feet into my flip-flops. That was easy. Then I brushed my hair using my left hand. That was *pretty* easy. Then I went downstairs.

"Why, Karen," Elizabeth exclaimed. "Who helped you get dressed? I thought Kristy was still asleep."

"She is," I replied. I sat down at the table. "I did it myself. I can do anything."

Elizabeth raised her eyebrows. She looked at Daddy.

"You can*not* do anything," said David

Michael. He and Andrew were sitting at the table with Daddy and Elizabeth.

"I can too." To prove it, I put a piece of bread in the toaster, left-handed. When it popped up, I buttered it, left-handed. The buttering took longer than usual — but I did it.

"See?" I said to David Michael.

David Michael stuck his tongue out at me.

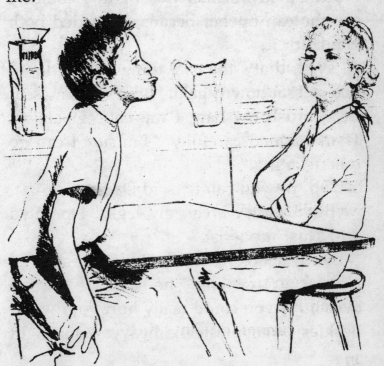

I stuck mine out at him.

"Okay, okay," said Daddy. "Karen, you must be feeling better."

"I'm fine!" I replied. I smiled. If I wanted to go roller-skating, I'd better look fine.

"I know one thing you can't do," said David Michael. "I bet you can't use the can opener, so you can't feed Boo-Boo."

"We'll see," I said, jumping up.

But David Michael was right. I couldn't use the can opener because I needed both hands for it.

"Well, that's the *only* thing I can't do," I said as I sat down again. "I can dress myself, I can brush my hair, I can eat." I paused. Then I added carefully. "I'm *sure* I can go roller-skating."

"Oh, no you can't!" said Daddy.

"But I didn't break my legs," I pointed out. "Just my wrist."

Daddy shook his head. "No roller-skating. Not for a long time," he said. "If you fell over now, you could really hurt your wrist. Besides, your plaster is heavy. You might not realize it, but you're off balance. Or you would be if you were on skates."

"Oh, *Daddy*," I said.

"Anyway," he went on, "you have to go back to hospital this morning. Doctor Humphrey wants to check your plaster. Tom might even take another X-ray."

"Back to *hospital*?" I cried. "I don't want to go!"

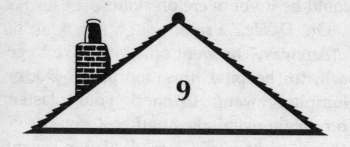

Waiting

I had to go back to hospital. I was very cross.

Daddy wanted to go straight away. "We don't have an appointment," he said. "We're just supposed to go to casualty this morning and wait until Doctor Humphrey can see you. If we go early, maybe we won't have to wait so long."

We left so early that Kristy was *still* asleep. Drat! I wanted her to come with us. She thinks up good games when you have to do a lot of waiting.

"Can I come?" asked Andrew.

"Well," said Daddy, "I suppose so. It's not going to be much fun, though. We'll just be sitting and waiting."

"I want to see a hospital," Andrew said. "Hospitals are instristing."

"Interesting," I corrected him.

"Can I go?" Andrew asked again.

"Yes," replied Daddy.

So Andrew came with us. Daddy drove to the hospital. This time he didn't have to park near the casualty department, and I could walk into the hospital by myself.

"Why are we going to casualty?" I asked Daddy. "I'm not an emergency now."

"Because Doctor Humphrey doesn't have a surgery like Doctor Dellenkamp does. He just mends bones, and he does it here in the hospital."

I nodded. Andrew and I sat down in hard plastic chairs in the waiting room. Daddy told the nurse we were there.

"WAHHH!"

Andrew and I turned around fast. Who was crying?

We saw a woman carrying a little girl through the doors under the EMERGENCY sign. The woman was running and the girl was screeching.

"She burned her hand!" the woman told a nurse.

The nurse grabbed some forms for the woman to sign. Then she took the lady and the little girl into one of those rooms with curtains for walls.

OOOO-EEEE-OOOO. An ambulance came speeding into the casualty car park. It pulled up to the doors of the hospital.

"Andrew! Look!" I cried.

Andrew and I ran to a window. We watched the back of the ambulance open up. Then three men and a woman lifted a stretcher out. They wheeled it inside in a hurry. It flew by us so fast we couldn't even see who was on the stretcher.

"Hey," I said. "Let's play hospital, Andrew. It will be a good waiting game."

"Okay. How do we play?"

"You be the sick person and I'll be the doctor," I told my brother. "You come to my hospital and I'll make you better."

"What's the matter with me?" asked Andrew.

"Whatever you want."

First Andrew had a broken leg.

"Hmm, I think you need a plastercast."

Andrew put his leg in my lap and I pretended to make a plastercast for it.

"Now I have a very very very very sore throat," said Andrew.

I looked down his throat. "You need this medicine," I told him. "It tastes horrid, but you have to take it seventeen times a day. Then your throat will get better."

"Thank you," said Andrew. "Now . . . now I have a big cut on my hand. It's bleeding."

"Yuck," I replied. "Okay. First we put some cream on it, and then a plaster. Then —"

"Karen Brewer?" said a nurse.

"She's here," Daddy answered. He and

Andrew and I stood up. Daddy held my unbroken hand.

Oh no! I thought. Doctor-time again.

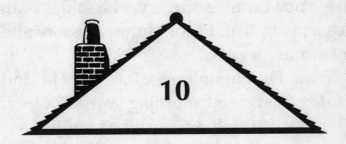

The Bone Doctor Again

The nurse showed Daddy and Andrew and me into one of the curtain rooms. Nearby I could hear the little girl with the burned hand crying.

"Come on Karen," said the nurse. "Sit right here on the table." She lifted me up.

"Do I have to have another injection?" I asked her nervously.

The nurse smiled. "No, not this time. Now just wait a few minutes and Doctor Humphrey will be in."

Daddy and Andrew sat down next to the

table. Andrew looked around him. "This is like a real doctor's surgery," he said. "I can see bandages and those funny scissors and medicine for cuts."

Then Dr Humphrey came in. He and Daddy said good morning to each other. Then Dr Humphrey looked at my plaster. He turned it over and around. "Does this hurt?" he kept asking.

"No . . . no . . . no . . . YES! OW!" I was very cross with the doctor for hurting me.

"Sorry," he said. "Karen, tell me how you broke your wrist."

"Well," I replied. "I was roller-skating down our road and I had arranged four empty coffee jars and I jumped over all of them. I landed perfectly." I paused. I knew that wasn't what had really happened, but I was too embarrassed to say that I fell over when I was just trying to turn round. After all, I was supposed to be a good skater. I didn't want people to think I couldn't even turn round without falling over. I decided to add something else to my story. "It was my best stunt ever. I even twirled round in the air," I said.

"Karen —" Andrew began.

"But," I went on, "just after I landed I saw a big caterpillar on the pavement."

"Caterpillar?" repeated Daddy. He frowned.

"I didn't want to squash it," I said, "so I tried to leap around it. But I lost my balance. My feet went out from under me, and I put

my hands out like this —" (I showed Dr Humphrey with my good hand)" — and I landed on them. And *crunch*, my right wrist broke."

"There weren't four jars," Andrew said, but no one heard him.

"Hmm," said Dr Humphrey. "That's the best way I can think of to break a wrist. Well, it's time for Tom to take some more pictures. We need to see if your bones are doing what they're supposed to be doing."

"More X-rays," I said. I sighed.

This time, Andrew came with me to visit Tom. Daddy stayed behind to talk to Dr Humphrey. When Tom had finished, a nurse took us back to Daddy. She handed my X-rays to the doctor.

Dr Humphrey clipped them to a lighted box. He looked at them for a long time. So did I. Funny black-and-white pictures. I could see the bones in my arm and all the bones in my fingers. (There were lots of them.)

"Well," said Dr Humphrey. "Hmm.

This is what I think will happen. For a couple of weeks, you'll come to out-patients every Wednesday afternoon. Tom will take X-rays. After two weeks, we'll remove this big plaster and we'll put a smaller one on. It will be lighter and more comfortable. Then you will only have to have X-rays once every two weeks. And eight weeks from now, we'll take your plaster off for good." Dr Humphrey smiled.

But I burst into tears. "Eight weeks!" I cried. "That's a long time."

"Well, yes it is," Daddy said. "It's two months."

I cried even harder. So Dr Humphrey gave me a Kleenex.

"I don't want to wear this for two months. I want to go roller-skating."

"Not until your wrist has healed," the doctor told me.

"That's awful!" I said as I blew my nose. Then I thought of something. "Will I be able to go to school?" I asked.

"Oh, yes. In a few days, your wrist won't

hurt at all. You'll be able to hold a pencil and write, even with the plaster on."

Drat. I'd been hoping for a holiday.

Yesterday, I thought, had been a bad day. But today was even worse. No roller-skating for two months — and I still had to go to school.

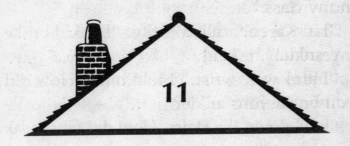

Ricky's Plastercast

"Goodbye, Karen!" Dr Humphrey called as Daddy and Andrew and I left.

" 'Bye," I replied glumly.

We walked back to the waiting room.

"Look, Karen. There's a boy with a plaster just like yours," said Andrew. "Only his is on his foot."

I was feeling very sorry for myself, so I was staring at the ground. But I glanced up, and then I opened my eyes wide.

"Daddy!" I whispered loudly. I tugged at his shirt, but I didn't point. Pointing isn't polite. "I know that boy! That's Ricky. He's in my class."

"Hi, Karen," called Ricky. "Look! I broke my ankle!" he said.

"I broke my wrist," I told him. "How did you break your ankle?"

"I fell down the stairs. How did you break your wrist?"

"Roller-skating."

Daddy and Andrew and I walked over to Ricky Torres and his parents. Daddy started talking to Mr and Mrs Torres. As he was busy, I said to Ricky, "I was doing a roller-skating stunt. I jumped over five jars lined up on the pavement. I did a double twist in the air. Then I landed. It was perfect." There. That was even better. I didn't want the other children in my class to know what had really happened.

"Karen," said Andrew.

I ignored him. "It was perfect except that I saw this caterpillar and her baby caterpillar and − Hey!"

I was so busy talking that I hadn't noticed

something important. Ricky's plaster was covered with people's names and funny sayings, all written with different pens. Ricky's plaster looked like an autograph book. I leaned over to see it better. Someone had written,

$$2 \text{ Ys U R,}$$
$$2 \text{ Ys U B,}$$
$$1 \text{ C U R}$$
$$2 \text{ Ys 4 me.}$$

"That's great!" I cried. "What's all this writing on your plaster? Who wrote it?"

"My friends and my mum and dad and brother and sister."

"But — but when did you break your ankle?" I asked. I couldn't work out how Ricky had had time to show his plaster to so many people.

"I broke it on Friday, after school."

Oh. Ricky had been able to show his plaster around all day Saturday.

"Is Doctor Humphrey your bone doctor?" I asked.

"Yes. Is he yours?"

"Yes. How long do you have to have your foot in plaster for?"

"Six weeks," said Ricky. "How about you?"

"Eight weeks. My broken bone must be worse than yours," I said proudly.

"I suppose so." Ricky narrowed his eyes. "I can't wait for school tomorrow. Everyone will want to see my plaster."

"Mine, too!" I cried. "They'll want to see mine, too!"

"But they'll want to see mine more," Ricky told me. "Mine is more interesting. And do you know what? By tomorrow morning, I will have Hubert Gregory's signature."

"The baseball player?!" I exclaimed. "He's famous! How are you going to get him to sign your plaster?"

"He's my dad's friend," said Ricky. He grinned at me, but I couldn't grin back.

"Well, we'd better be going," said Daddy. "Karen, say goodbye to Ricky."

" 'Bye, Ricky."

" 'Bye, Karen."

Gosh, I thought, I had plenty to do that afternoon. I had to get lots of people to sign my plaster. I couldn't let Ricky go to school with a better plaster than mine. But how could I get a signature that was as good as Hubert Gregory's? I didn't know anyone famous.

"Daddy," I said as we were driving home, "I'm going to be very busy this afternoon."

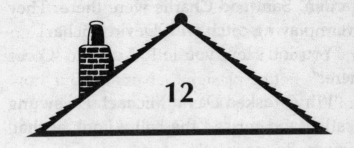

12

Karen's Plastercast

"Hey, everybody!" I called when we got home. "Elizabeth! Kristy! Charlie! Sa —"

"Karen, don't shout so loudly," said Daddy.

"But this is important," I told him. "I need people to sign my plaster."

"Well, go and find them, darling," said Daddy. "Look. Here's a red pen." He pulled a pen out of his shirt pocket and gave it to me. "Take this with you, but calm down. There's no need to yell."

I tried to calm down. "Thank you," I said

61

as I took the pen. I went into our back garden. Sam and Charlie were there. They were playing catch with David Michael.

"You lot! Hey, you lot!" I called. "Come here!"

"Why?" asked David Michael. He swung his bat and missed the ball. "Look at that! You made me miss!"

"Did not!" I cried. "Now come here. I want you to sign my plaster."

"Really?" said David Michael. My brothers looked interested. They dropped their gloves and the bat and ball and came over to me. I gave Sam my pen.

"Can you write your name or something funny or draw a picture?" I asked him as I took off my sling.

"Of course," replied Sam. He thought for a moment. Then he wrote,

Yours till the banana splits. Ha, ha, ha! Sam

I giggled.

Sam gave the pen to Charlie, and Charlie wrote,

> Roses are red,
> cabbages are green,
> my face is funny,
> but yours is a scream.
> Your brother Charlie.

I stuck my tongue out at him. But I couldn't help laughing.

"David Michael?" I asked.

David Michael looked very thoughtful. After a long pause he wrote,

GET WELL SOON.
DAVID MICHAEL THOMAS.

"That's great!" I cried. "Thanks a lot. By the way, do you know anyone famous?"

My brothers shook their heads, so I went to look for the rest of my family.

First I found Kristy, and she wrote,

Roses are red,
violets are blue.
sugar is sweet,
and so are you!
Love, Kristy

Then I found Andrew, and he wrote,

ANDREW

Then I found Daddy, and he wrote,

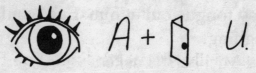

The autographs were great, but Daddy didn't know anyone famous, and neither did Kristy or Andrew.

At last I found Elizabeth. I gave her the red pen. She wrote,

YOURS TILL ICE SCREAMS!
LOVE, ELIZABETH

"Thank you," I said, "Do you know anyone famous?"

Elizabeth frowned. "I don't think so, darling. Why?"

I told her about Ricky and his plaster and Hubert Gregory.

"Oh," said Elizabeth. "I see." She paused. "Hey, I've got an idea! Come with me, and take off your sling on the way."

I followed Elizabeth into the study. First she got an ink pad. Then she got some tissues. Then she tiptoed over to the sofa. Shannon and Boo-Boo were lying there asleep.

Very carefully, Elizabeth lifted Boo-Boo's

front paw. She opened the ink pad and pressed Boo-Boo's foot onto it.

"HISSSSSS!" went Boo-Boo. He didn't like being disturbed.

But quick as a flash, Elizabeth put Boo-Boo's foot on my plaster. It left a pawprint!

"There's Boo-Boo's autograph," she said, as she cleaned his foot. "Boo-Boo isn't famous, but that's a pretty special autograph."

I smiled at Boo-Boo's pawprint.

Then Elizabeth got Shannon's autograph the same way — except that Shannon slept through the whole thing.

Two pawprints. "Thanks!" I cried. "That's great, Elizabeth!"

Only I knew that the pawprints weren't *quite* as good as Hubert Gregory's signature. They were good — but not good enough.

I still needed a really really really special autograph.

Where would I get it?

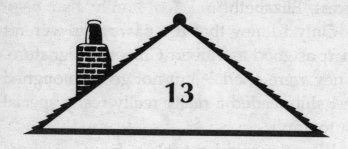

Karen's Story Grows

I decided I would have to go and visit people. I needed lots of people to sign my plaster, anyway. I would ask our neighbours to do it. Then I would ask them if they knew anyone famous.

"Elizabeth? May I go over to Hannie's? And then maybe to Amanda Delaney's? I need some more autographs on my plaster."

"Yes," replied Elizabeth. "Just be careful. And come home if you're tired or if your arm starts to hurt."

"Okay. Thanks!"

68

I ran across the street to the Papadakises' house. Hannie and her family had been away the day before. Hannie *would* be surprised when she saw me.

"Karen!" Hannie cried when she opened her door. "What happened?"

"I broke my wrist," I said proudly.

"Hey, everyone! Come here!" Hannie called.

Hannie's parents and her brother, Linny, came running. They all wanted to hear about my accident. So I told them the story.

"I was showing Andrew a new stunt," I said. But suddenly, five coffee jars didn't sound like enough. Not enough for a broken wrist, anyway. "I arranged seven coffee jars on the pavement," I went on. "Then I went a long way away from them. I skated towards the jars so fast I was almost flying. I sailed over them. . . . I *was* flying! Just for a second. And I did a triple twist in the air. Then I landed."

"And that's when you fell?" asked Linny.

"No. Not then," I said. "I landed perfectly.

But in front of me I saw a mother caterpillar and her three babies." (That sounded pretty good!) "I didn't want to squash the babies, so I tried to jump over them, too. *That* was when I fell." (Mr and Mrs Papadakis frowned, but they didn't say anything.)

"Did you fall on the caterpillars?" asked Hannie.

"What? Oh. Oh, no. They were safe," I said quickly. "Would you like to sign my plaster? All of you? I need autographs on it. Look, even Shannon and Boo-Boo have signed it." I took off my sling and held out my arm so the Papadakises could look at the plaster.

"I'll go and get a pen!" Hannie cried.

"Get one that isn't red," I told her. I wanted my cast to look as colourful as Ricky's.

Hannie and Linny and their mother and father signed my plaster.

"I suppose Sari is too little to sign it, isn't she?" I said. (Sari is the littlest Papadakis.)

"Yes," agreed Mrs Papadakis. "But how would you like another pawprint? I think we could get Noodle's autograph." (Noodle is a poodle.)

"Thank you very much," I said when Noodle had finished. "By the way, does anyone here know a famous person?"

"No," said Hannie and Linny.

"I know the dogcatcher," said Mr Papadakis.

I shook my head.

"I know the mayor," said Mrs Papadakis.

"You *do*?" I cried. "Could he sign my plaster? I need a famous autograph before tomorrow."

"Oh," said Hannie's mother. "I'm sorry, Karen. He's away this weekend."

"That's okay," I answered in a small voice.

"Hey, Karen! How about a *claw*print? That would be good!" exclaimed Hannie. "We'll get Myrtle to sign your cast. A turtle's autograph!"

It wasn't easy, but Hannie and Linny put Myrtle's clawprint on my cast.

When they had finished, I said, "Thanks, everybody. I have to go now. I'm going to ask some more people to sign my plaster. Do you want to come with me, Hannie?"

"Where are you going first?"

"Over to Amanda Delaney's."

"Karen Brewer! How could you do that to me?" Hannie cried, "You know Amanda and I are VERY BIG ENEMIES!"

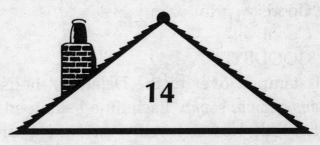

Karen's Story Grows Some More

Hannie Papadakis hardly ever gets angry and she hardly ever yells. But it's true: she doesn't like Amanda, and Amanda doesn't like her. Amanda can make Hannie angry.

"I'm sorry, Hannie," I said. "I need Amanda to sign my plaster. And Max and their mum and dad."

Hannie was walking me to the front door. "Well, I'm not going!" she said.

I began to feel angry, too. "Okay! Then don't!"

"I won't!"

"Good!"

"Goodbye!"

"GOODBYE!"

I stamped over to the Delaneys' house. *Stamp, stamp, stamp.* Each time I stamped, I felt a little less angry. By the time I rang Amanda's door, I wasn't angry at all. I even wished Hannie had come with me. It's very silly of her not to like Amanda. And it's silly of Amanda not to like Hannie.

When I rang Amanda's bell, Shannon Kilbourne answered the door. Shannon lives in the house between Hannie and Amanda. Shannon is a babysitter, just like Kristy. (She gave us our dog, and that's why we named the puppy Shannon, after Shannon Kilbourne.)

"Hi, Shannon," I said. "Are you babysitting for Amanda and Max?"

"Yes, I am. Karen, what happened to your arm?" Shannon asked.

So I had to tell the story again. Shannon invited me into Amanda and Max's

74

playroom, and I told them that I had jumped over ten coffee jars, and that I had broken my wrist and the police had had to come, and an ambulance as well.

I love telling stories. And this one was getting to be one of my best. No one would ever know that I had fallen just by trying to turn round.

When I had finished, I said, "Will you sign my plaster?"

"Yes," replied Amanda and Max and Shannon.

Amanda wrote:

Read	see	that	me.
up	will	I	love
and	you	love	you
down	and	you	and

"Great!" I cried.

Then Shannon wrote,

Best wishes from Shannon Kilbourne

And Max, who is six, wrote,

Hi FROM MAX.

"Thanks," I said. "By the way, Shannon and Boo-Boo and Noodle put their pawprints on my plaster. And Myrtle put her clawprint on it. Maybe Priscilla could sign my plaster too." Priscilla is the Delaneys' fluffy white cat.

"How did you get their pawprints?" asked Amanda.

"With an ink pad," I told her.

"Ink? No way! I don't want Priscilla's paw getting dirty."

I sighed. "Okay," I said. "Hey, do any of you know anyone famous?"

"Why?" asked Shannon.

"I need someone famous to sign my plaster," I answered. "By tomorrow. It's important."

"I don't know anyone," said Amanda.

"Me neither," said Shannon.

But Max said, "There's a boy in my class

whose aunt has a friend who goes to a hairdresser who once cut Frances Morton's hair."

"Who's Frances Morton?" I asked.

"A singer," said Max. "I think."

"Are you sure the hairdresser cut her hair?"

"No," admitted Max.

"Well," I said, "thank you. But your friend probably couldn't sign my plaster before tomorrow. Besides, it would be better if Frances Morton could sign my plaster herself."

"Hey!" Amanda shouted. "Guess what! I hear bells! Mr Softee is coming!"

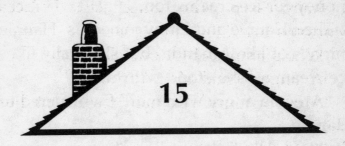

15

Mr Softee

"Hooray!" I cried. "The ice-cream man! And I have fifty cents with me!"

"Can we have money for ice-creams, Shannon?" asked Amanda.

And Max added, "*Please*?"

Shannon gave Amanda and Max some money and we ran across the Delaneys' lawn. We stopped at the pavement. We could see Mr Softee's van a few houses away. We could hear it, too. The bells were ringing and music was playing. Over the road my front door opened. Andrew and

David Michael ran out and I knew they had money for ice-creams too.

Then Hannie and Linny joined us. Hannie might not like Amanda, but she really likes ice-cream so she stood with us.

"Are you angry with me?" I whispered to Hannie.

"Not really," she replied. "Are you angry with me?"

"No."

We smiled at each other.

Mr Softee drove slowly down the street. Just in case he didn't see us, we all began waving our arms. We yelled, "Stop! Stop here, Mr Softee!"

Jangle, *jangle* went the bells. The van stopped right beside us and Mr Softee looked out.

"Karen Brewer!" he exclaimed. "What on earth did you do to yourself?"

I giggled. Mr Softee is really nice. He always stops and talks to us, and we love him.

I told Mr Softee how I broke my wrist. I

told him an even better story than I'd told Shannon and Amanda and Max. The new story had helicopters and fire engines in it. When I got to that part, I realized something. Everyone was staring at me. Mr Softee's mouth was open. "Karen," he said, "are you *sure* that's what happened?"

"No, it's not!" said Andrew. "That's a very big story. There were only two coffee jars. And there were no caterpillars or ambulances or police cars or fire engines or helicopters."

Now everyone was staring at Andrew. He hardly ever talks so much.

At last Amanda said, "Why don't you tell us the truth, Karen?"

So I did. It wasn't nearly as interesting, but nobody seemed to mind. And nobody laughed at me. They were much more interested in my plaster and in the autographs than in how I'd fallen over.

Then I said, "Mr Softee, could I have a Feast, please?"

Andrew asked for a Cornetto, David

Michael asked for an orange ice lolly, Hannie and Linny asked for chocolate ice-cream cones, and Amanda and Max asked for mini milks.

We paid Mr Softee. Just before he drove off, I had an idea.

"Mr Softee, would you sign my plaster, please?" I asked him.

Mr Softee found a pen. He wrote,

TO KAREN,
ONE OF MY BEST CUSTOMERS.
BEST WISHES,
ROGER JONES

"Roger Jones!" I cried. "Don't you mean . . . Isn't your name Mr Softee?"

"Roger Softee?" asked Mr Softee. He was smiling. "I'm sorry, Karen. Mr Softee is just the name of the ice-cream company."

"Oh." I blushed. Then I said, "Could you write Mr Softee underneath your name? Just so people will know who Roger Jones is?" I asked.

"Okay," said Mr Softee. He got his pen out again. "There you go." Then he drove off.

My friends and brothers and I looked at each other. We couldn't believe that Mr Softee was really Roger Jones.

And I said, "It's not fair. I still don't have a special autograph."

"What about Mr Softee's?" said David Michael.

I frowned. "I'm not sure. Ricky might have his too. And *drat!* I forgot to ask Mr Softee if he knows anyone famous."

The afternoon was not going as well as I wanted it to.

I needed to do some thinking.

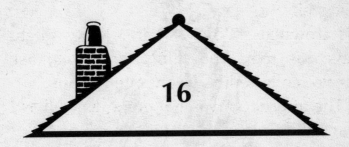

Eek! Morbidda Destiny!

My friends and brothers and I sat down on the kerb. We licked our ice-creams and as we sat, I thought.

I looked across the street. I saw the place where I had fallen. I saw our garage, where my skates were. They would be stuck in the garage for weeks and weeks. Then I saw . . . Morbidda Destiny, the witch next door!

"Eek! There's Morbidda Destiny!" I whispered loudly.

Everyone looked over at her house.

"I bet she's gathering herbs for a spell," I said softly.

"What kind of spell?" asked Andrew. His voice was trembling.

"I don't know. Something awful. Maybe a spell to take away Christmas."

"A spell to take away *Christmas*?" howled Max. "No!"

"SHH!" I said. "Isn't it just my luck that I have to live next door to a witch? I'm sure she's the only witch in Stoneybrook. And she lives — Hey! That's it!" I cried. Then I lowered my voice. I didn't want the witch to hear me. "That's it," I said more softly.

"That's what?" asked David Michael.

"Nothing," I answered. I was busy thinking. I could get Morbidda Destiny to sign my plaster. Ricky wouldn't have a *witch's* autograph. And a witch's autograph would be better than Hubert Gregory's any day.

Hmm. How could I *get* the witch's autograph, though? I would have to go to her house, or at least into her garden. I would have to stand near her. She would have to touch my plaster. Was I brave enough to do that?

Of course I was. . . . Well, I would be, if someone came with me. Someone like Hannie Papadakis. That was all I needed — a friend.

"Hannie?" I said. "Do you want to come over for a while?"

"Yes," replied Hannie. I could tell she

was glad I hadn't asked Amanda to come over, too.

Hannie and I stood up. We were still licking our ice-creams.

"See you later," I said.

"See you," said Andrew, David Michael, Linny, Max and Amanda.

"I'm glad you're not angry with me any more," I said to Hannie as we crossed the street.

"I'm glad, too," replied Hannie.

"Since we're friends again, will you help me do something?"

"What do you need help for?" asked Hannie.

"I want you to come over to Morbidda Destiny's with me."

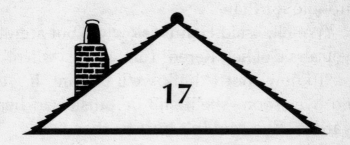

Lucky Charms

"No!" cried Hannie. Then she whispered, "I am *not* going to the witch's house again. The last time we went over there we got into very big trouble."

That was true. But that was because we did something wrong. "We won't do anything wrong this time," I told Hannie. We reached my house. We let ourselves inside and went to my room. "In fact, we're going to do something nice. We're going to ask Mor — Mrs Porter for her autograph. Don't you think that will make her happy?

She will think we like her. We won't get in trouble for that."

"We-ell," said Hannie slowly. "But aren't you afraid of her, Karen? I am. She's a witch."

"I know. But I think we'll be safe. If we go over soon, she'll still be outside in her garden. She couldn't hurt us then."

"Why not?" asked Hannie.

"Because everyone would see. Andrew and David Michael and Linny and Max and Amanda are across the road. The witch won't do anything with people watching. I know she won't."

"Maybe not," said Hannie.

"Don't you want me to have the best plaster in our class tomorrow?" I asked.

"Yes."

"Then will you help me?"

Hannie sighed. "Yes."

"Okay, now we have to think about how we're going to ask Morbidda Destiny for her autograph."

"Can't you just say, 'Please sign my plaster'?" suggested Hannie.

"What if she wants to know *why* I want her to sign my plaster? I can't tell her it's because she's a witch."

"Then say it's because . . . it's because . . . Oh, I don't know, Karen. You'll think of something, won't you?"

"I suppose so," I replied. I usually do.

"I don't know why I'm helping you," said Hannie. She made a face.

"I do. Because you're my friend."

Hannie and I smiled at each other.

"Now," I said, "we'd better protect ourselves while we're next door. We need some lucky charms. Just in case. I'll put my lucky rabbit's foot in my pocket. And you can put . . . let's see. You can put my lucky stone in your pocket."

The stone I keep in my desk drawer isn't really lucky. It's just pretty, but if Hannie *believed* it was lucky, that was probably all that mattered. So I told her it was a lucky stone. "Then we'll be safe," I added. I gave Hannie the stone. "Ready?" I asked.

"I hope so," Hannie replied.

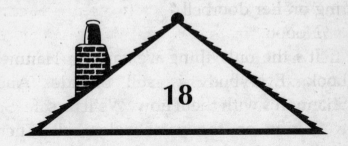

The Witch's Autograph

Hannie and I finished our ice-creams. Then we left our house. My hand was closed around the rabbit's foot. Hannie's was closed around the stone.

"Keep your hand on the stone all the time," I warned Hannie. "I'll keep — Uh-oh." I looked around nervously.

"What's wrong?" asked Hannie in a squeaky voice.

"That." I pointed to Morbidda Destiny's garden. It was empty. "She's gone," I said.

"She's probably inside now. We'll have to ring on her doorbell."

"Noooo."

"It's the only thing we can do, Hannie. Look. Everybody is still outside. And Shannon's with them now. We'll be safe. So we'll ring on the witch's doorbell. Then we'll stand on her porch and when she answers the door, I'll ask for her autograph. Simple. We won't go inside or anything."

"All right."

We walked out of my garden. We walked into Morbidda Destiny's. Her big old house stood before us. Very slowly, we climbed the porch steps. I looked at Hannie. Her hand was still in her pocket. "Are you holding the stone?" I asked.

She nodded.

"Good. Hold it tight. I'm holding the rabbit's foot. Our lucky charms will protect us."

I rang on Morbidda Destiny's doorbell. My hand was shaking.

After a moment, Hannie and I heard footsteps inside.

94

"Yes?" called a wobbly voice.

"It's us!" I said. "It's Karen Brewer and Hannie Papadakis."

The door opened slightly. Hannie and I could see a squinty eye and a pointy nose.

Then the door opened the rest of the way.

There stood my witch. She looked the same as always. She was wearing a long black dress. It came right to the top of her black shoes. Her grey hair was flying all over the place.

"Well," she said, "what can I do for you girls?"

I took off my sling and held out my arm. "I broke my wrist," I said timidly. "Would you, um, would you please sign my plaster?"

"How did you break it?" Morbidda Destiny asked.

"I was skating and I fell over," I told her.

The witch nodded. She didn't look impressed.

"I know it isn't very interesting," I said, "but that's what happened."

"Why do you want my autograph?" asked Morbidda Destiny.

"Because you're my neighbour," I said. I said it just as Hannie said, "Because she's in a plaster-signing contest."

Morbidda Destiny looked confused, but all she said was, "Let's see here." She reached into the folds of her dress. As if by magic, she pulled out a pen. Where had that pen been hiding?

The witch reached for my arm. I shut my eyes. I felt as if I was at the doctor's, waiting for an injection. Suddenly I was terrified. What was I doing? Was I crazy, letting a witch sign my plaster? Maybe if I pulled my arm away right then —

"There we go!" exclaimed Morbidda Destiny. She smiled happily.

Oh, no! She had already signed my plaster! I dared to open my eyes. What would I see? What would a witch put on a plaster?

In big black letters were the words "Tabitha Porter". Next to them was a drawing of a black cat. A black cat! Why had she drawn that? What was it? A spell? Maybe it was an awful sign that would attract other witches. What a horrible thought. But I couldn't do anything about it.

I had a witch's name and a witch's cat on my plaster now. It was time to go.

"Th-thanks, Mrs Porter!" I cried.

Then I grabbed Hannie's hand and we ran to my house.

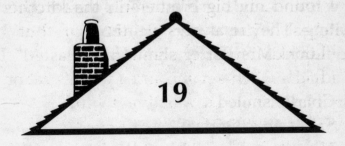

19

Home Safely

Hannie and I slammed the front door behind us. We were breathing very hard. We didn't say a word. After a few moments, I went into the living room. I turned on a light. I was going to examine what Morbidda Destiny had written.

Just then I heard Charlie call, "Karen? Is that you?"

"Yes!" I yelled back. I was shaking. But I said to Hannie, "Let's show everyone the witch's autograph." If no one else seemed worried about the black cat, then I wouldn't be worried either, I decided.

I found my big brothers in the kitchen, eating. They're always eating.

"Look! Mrs Porter signed my plaster!" I said.

Charlie smiled.

Sam said, "Big deal."

Hannie and I went into the back garden. Daddy and Elizabeth were gardening. Kristy was helping them. "Look!" I said again. "Mrs Porter signed my plaster!"

Daddy and Elizabeth and Kristy put down their trowels. They took off their gardening gloves. Then they stood up.

"You went over to Mrs Porter's?" exclaimed Kristy. "I thought you were afraid of her."

Daddy and Elizabeth were peering at my plaster.

"Very nice," said Daddy. "She even drew a picture of Midnight."

Oh! Midnight! So that's what the picture was. I felt very silly . . . and very relieved.

"I'm sure Mrs Porter was happy that you

wanted her autograph," added Elizabeth. "She's so lonely. Visits from children must mean a lot to her."

"Well, really," Hannie began, "we needed the autograph of a wi —"

"Of all our neighbours," I interrupted loudly. Daddy and Elizabeth wouldn't be happy if they knew Hannie and I were calling Mrs Porter a witch again. "Come on, Hannie. Let's go and count my autographs."

I pulled Hannie into the house. Phew!

"Hannie," I said, "you can't tell grown-ups about witches. Especially about Mrs Porter. They don't understand."

"Oh," replied Hannie.

We went back to the lamp in the living room.

"Tabitha Porter," I said, looking at the autograph. "A witchy-sounding name. Still, I wish Mrs Porter had written 'Morbidda Destiny' so everyone would know it was the autograph of my witch."

"Well, I'll tell them," said Hannie. "I was with you. I know."

"Thank you," I replied.

I was happy at last. Maybe my plaster wouldn't be better than Ricky's, but it would be just as good.

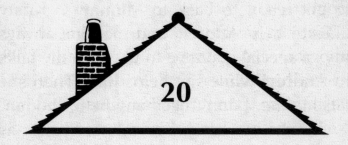

Goodbyes and Hellos

"Karen!" Kristy called.

"What?" I shouted. Hannie and I were still in the living room. We had been counting autographs.

"It's time for you and Andrew to get ready to go home."

"All right," I said. I sighed. I had lost count.

So had Hannie. She decided to leave.

" 'Bye!" I called. "See you in school tomorrow. Thank you for helping me."

Kristy found Andrew outside. She brought

him in. Then she brought both of us upstairs to get ready to back to Mummy's. Kristy likes to help Andrew and me. She always says a special goodbye to us. First she talks to Andrew while she helps him. Then she talks to me. I don't need any help, though.

"What a weekend, Karen," said Kristy as she came into my room.

"It was exciting, wasn't it?" I replied.

Kristy laughed. "I'll say! Think of everything that happened."

"I got a witch's autograph."

"You got a witch's autograph? How about having an accident? Breaking your wrist? And going to hospital — twice?"

"Getting X-rays," I added. "Meeting Tom. Meeting a bone doctor. Sitting in a wheelchair. And seeing Ricky and *his* plaster."

"That's right," said Kristy. "But do you know what? We don't want to have this kind of excitement too often."

"I wouldn't mind. When I go to school tomorrow, I'll be a star."

"You'll be a co-star," Kristy reminded me. "Ricky has a plaster too, so he'll be another star."

"Oh yes."

"Come on," said Kristy. "Your mum will be here any minute."

Andrew and I got our bags. We went downstairs to wait. Soon Mummy and Seth drove into Daddy's drive.

"Goodbye! Goodbye!" Andrew and I called to Daddy and Elizabeth and Kristy and Sam and Charlie and David Michael and Shannon and Boo-Boo. It took us a long time to hug everybody.

Then we ran to Mummy and Seth. "Hello! Hello!" we called. We kissed them as we climbed into the car. Their car was full of suitcases and things from their trip to Maine.

"My poor Karen!" exclaimed Mummy when she saw my cast and sling.

"My arm hardly hurts at all," I told her. "And look. Look at all the autographs on my cast. Now you and Seth have got to sign it."

Mummy was driving, so Seth signed my cast. He wrote

U R 2 nice
2 B 4- gotten.
            Love,
                 Seth

Mummy said, "I'll sign your plaster at home, darling. Hey, how would you like the autograph of someone famous? My friend

106

Amy Morris is in Stoneybrook this weekend. Maybe we could visit her tonight."

"Amy Morris the film star?!" I shrieked. "She's a friend of yours? And she's *here*?"

"Yes," said Mummy, laughing.

I couldn't believe it. I just couldn't believe it. I went looking for someone famous and didn't find anybody. Then I stopped looking and found somebody. Oh, well. Whether we saw Amy Morris or not, I would still be the only person with a *witch's* autograph.

I smiled. It hadn't been such a bad weekend after all.